# Claiming Ivy

## Claiming series
### Book 1

## Violet Rae

# Blurb

**She's off-limits, but one night together could change everything... if he's willing to risk it all.**

**Ivy**

I've been in love with my father's best friend since I was eighteen, but I know I don't even register on his radar—until one night when he steps in to deal with a bitter ex-boyfriend hellbent on teaching me a lesson.

**Ashton**

I've hidden my feelings from Ivy for years—after all, she's forbidden fruit. Right? Taking her home with me may not be my best decision ever because once she's in my bed... all bets are off.

*Plot? Basically just smut. No apologies.* 😉

- *Dad's best friend.*

- *Older man, younger woman.*

- *Virgin heroine.*

- *Celibate hero.*

- *No cheating*

- *HEA*

- *Smutty-smut-smut (yeah, that's a new trope I made up 😊)*

# Chapter 1
# Ivy

Ashton Stanbrook is a pain in my ass.

He leans casually against the wall by the drawing-room door, his arms crossed over his broad chest, a smile pulling at his mouth as he listens to Mom's speech.

"I'd like to thank everyone for coming here tonight. It's a double celebration as not only is it Ivy's twenty-first birthday, but she's also graduated college early." Mom beams at the guests gathered around in the large drawing room.

It's the happiest I've seen her since Dad died. For months she's been telling me I need to get my head out of the clouds and focus on my future. I tend to be a bit of a daydreamer, which I know drives her crazy at times.

She's a fantastic defense lawyer, so she's practical and organized at all times—unlike me. I'm messy and disorganized, the one who's always running late or forgetting where I'm supposed to be. It's a miracle that I've graduated with my short attention span—and not only graduated but graduated early.

However, something has held my attention span for longer than a nanosecond—or rather, some*one*.

*Ashton.*

A man I've wanted since before I even knew what wanting was. I mean, what's not to like about him? He's caring, rugged, and handsome, with his dark hair, blue eyes, and tall, muscular body.

I can't help what I feel for him. The childish daydreams I had about him during my youth became much more grown-up, and by the time I hit eighteen, I could barely string a sentence together in his presence.

He's always looked out for Mom and me, especially since Dad died five years ago. He took care of everything, from the legal paperwork to the funeral arrangements. I don't know what we would've done without him. I was sixteen then. Maybe that's when I began to see him as a man rather than a mentor.

I remember watching him one day as he mowed the lawn for us. It was hot that day, and he peeled off his t-shirt, giving me a delicious view of his broad shoulders and tight abs.

I've been half in love with him for as long as I can remember. I've gone all out tonight, wearing an emerald-blue designer dress that flatters my plus-size figure. It clings to my generous boobs, skims my waist, and lands in silky folds above my knees.

My long, blonde hair falls in a golden curtain halfway down my back, and my makeup is on point. For once, not only do I look sexy, I feel sexy too. And all my efforts are for one man.

A man who's barely given me the time of day in recent months. Something shifted between us that night—the night he passed by my bedroom door on my eighteenth birthday and saw me in my underwear.

He hesitated in the doorway, but instead of trying to cover myself up, I turned to face him, letting him see me. His eyes narrowed possessively, raking down my body, taking in his fill. That look set every nerve ending in my body on fire, and I found myself arching my body slightly, tempting him. I knew it was wrong, but at that moment, it felt so right.

Things haven't been the same between us since.

Two weeks later, I was off to an exclusive college a thousand miles away. I've only seen Ashton a handful of times since the night of my eighteenth birthday, and he's seemed more remote each time.

College was tough, and studying for my Associate Nursing degree kept me busy. It was also a world away from the small town I grew up in, protected and sheltered by my parents. I was shy and a little geeky, but I came into my own at college.

I started buying clothes that flattered my full figure and put myself out there socially. I was finally becoming familiar with who I was outside the confines of my upbringing.

Some boys showed interest once I improved my image a little. It was flattering to have some male attention for the first time in my life, but pleasant as those boys were, I couldn't help but think of them as precisely that—boys.

I dated one guy, Brent, my best friend Clara's brother, but it didn't last long. There was no way I could be intimate with him. Not his fault—he wasn't Ashton.

"She's not my little girl anymore. She's a grown woman ready to take the world by storm," Mom is saying, her loving gaze settling on me. "I wish your father were here to see you now, honey. He'd be so proud." Her voice breaks, and she dabs at her eyes. She raises her glass of champagne. "To Ivy!"

"To Ivy!" the guests chant in unison, raising their glasses and bottles of beer.

My eyes slide to Ashton as if drawn there by an invisible thread, and my stomach flips as I find his intense gaze fixed on me. The sight of him makes me tingle all over. He raises his glass slightly in a toast, a smile tugging up one corner of his mouth.

He's far too hot for his own good. Broad shoulders, narrow waist, muscular thighs. He was my dad's best friend, and after his sudden death from a heart attack five years ago, Ashton swooped in and took care of everything. I don't know what Mom and I would've done without him.

Maybe that's when I began to notice him as a man rather than as Dad's best friend. But I'm twenty-one to his thirty-nine. It makes no difference to me, but I'm sure it's a deal-breaker for him. After all, I'm still his best friend's daughter, even if Dad is no longer with us.

But I'm fooling myself, thinking someone like me can capture the attention of a man like him. He still thinks of me as a child, not the woman who's been half in love with him since I was sixteen. He's behind every one of my fantasies. It's his face I picture when I touch myself alone in my bed at night and his name that spills from my lips as I get myself off.

I may wish things were different, but I know I'm off-limits in every conceivable way as far as Ashton Stanbrook is concerned.

# Chapter 2
# Ashton

"I'd like to thank everyone for coming here tonight. It's a double celebration as not only is it Ivy's twenty-first birthday, but she's also graduated college early," Kathy beams at the guests gathered around in the large drawing room at the three-story townhouse.

She looks happy, maybe the happiest I've seen her since Jack, her husband, and my best friend, died. Pride shines from her face as she mentions her daughter, and a whole shit-storm of emotions hits me.

*Ivy.*

The daughter of my two best friends.

Tonight is her party to celebrate her twenty-first birthday and graduation, her coming-of-age. And damned if the way she keeps looking at me doesn't prove she's all grown up. No longer off-limits. Everything inside me wants her, wants to own her, possess her.

She's a woman now, and, Jesus, fuck, she's hot. Somehow, cute little Ivy has grown into the most desirable woman I've ever laid eyes on. She's all plush tits and wild curves with an ass I want to palm and squeeze as I fuck her.

She's *womanly and* walks around like she has no fucking clue how tempting she is. She's also clumsy and disorganized, but she has a rare determination and intelligence for her age. There's a freshness, a youthfulness that clings to her, but she's also got a good head on her shoulders. Losing her father probably had something to do with that when she was sixteen. She had to grow up quicker than most girls her age.

A natural caregiver, she's now completed her Associate Nursing Degree, and I know, without a shadow of a doubt, she'll be amazing in her chosen career.

How can I interfere with that? With her plans for her future? There are so many reasons I can't, I *shouldn't*, claim her as mine, but it's getting harder and harder to remember a single fucking one of them.

Especially tonight, when she looks like a dream in an ocean-blue dress that transforms her into a goddess. It skims all her delicious curves while emphasizing her magnificent tits and rounded ass.

At eighteen years her senior, I'm too goddamn old for her, but there's something about Ivy that has me as hard as fucking steel. And *that* is a real problem.

It didn't happen overnight. My feelings for her slowly started to change right before her eighteenth birthday. I hugged her that night, lifting her off her feet as I held her close, her warm body and soft skin under my hands. Her whole face lit up when she was in my arms, and as I pulled away, something passed between us, primal and needy.

Then, later that evening, I glimpsed her in her underwear as I passed her bedroom on the way to the bathroom. Her door was ajar as she removed her dress. She didn't shy away from my eyes as I paused outside her door, held immobile by the sight of her in a silk bra and panties. No, she turned to me, letting me look my fill, her back arching slightly, her eyes drowsy with desire.

And what did I do? I walked away. Hardest fucking thing I've ever done.

Maybe I should've claimed her that night, but I had to let her spread her wings and experience a little of life first, even if it was in the sheltered confines of an exclusive college. If she came back to me after that? Well, then, all bets were off.

"To Ivy!"

"To Ivy!" the guests raise their glasses and bottles of beer in unison.

I glance across at Ivy to find her golden-brown eyes fixed on me. My heart skips, and my dick throbs at the look in those tawny eyes. I raise my glass an inch, silently toasting her, giving her what I hope is a cool smile while my insides turn to lava.

My self-control is slipping where she's concerned, and I'm dangerously close to the precipice. One nudge, and I know I'll be tumbling face-first over the edge and straight into Ivy's arms.

# Chapter 3
# Ivy

Mom swoops in, pulling my attention away from Ashton as she grabs me for a hug. "I'm so proud of you, honey," she says huskily, still dabbing at her tears. She's a tough cookie, and it's rare for anyone other than me to witness her shedding tears.

She's earned a fierce reputation in her field of work and is constantly sought after for high-profile cases. Like tomorrow, for example, when she leaves for New York to defend a well-known celebrity accused of beating up his girlfriend.

Another guest steals Mom away, so I spend the next hour doing the rounds, talking with the family and friends who've come to help me celebrate. Clara, my best friend from college, arrives a little later, saving me from an awkward conversation with some distant family cousin. I may have recently earned my nursing degree, but it doesn't mean I want to hear all about the skin tags he has growing on his scrotum.

However, Clara isn't alone, and I'm surprised that Brent is with her. She's obviously brought him as her plus one, which seems odd. We only dated a few times, so we were never officially boyfriend and girlfriend. We didn't end on the best of terms, though. He had feelings for me that I couldn't return because I was pining for someone else.

Clara and I catch up for a little while before she heads for the buffet table, leaving me alone with Brent. I'm expecting things to be awkward, but if anything, he seems overly attentive as we talk. He touches me at every opportunity as he refills my wine glass, asking me about my plans now I've graduated. I try to focus on answering his questions, but my attention is half-hearted at best.

I need to move past this obsession with Ashton.

Maybe I'll join a dating site. But how many men are looking to date an overweight virgin? Besides, the thought of being intimate with anyone except Ashton is wrong. Not to mention, Mom would probably have a coronary. She wants me to be independent, but she also thinks the world is full of predators who will club me over the head, drag me back to their cave, and make me their sexual prisoner. Somehow, that doesn't sound like such a horrible idea with Ashton on the other end of the club.

The evening drags on. The more I try to ignore Ashton, the more aware I am of him. Every time my eyes find him, he's already watching me with a frown. I can't help but notice Rebecca, one of Mom's divorced friends, is sniffing around him. The sight of her pawing at him makes my stomach churn. Pretty sure I've heard Mom moan about her being high-maintenance, which is one of the reasons she's divorced. The other being she was banging the guy next door.

I deliberately move to the other end of the room to escape the sight of them, but seconds later, Ashton has closed the space between us again, Rebecca trailing on his heels.

I'm done. I need a few minutes to myself. I've drunk more alcohol than I usually do, and I'm a little dizzy and nauseous. The room is suddenly too hot, and I need some fresh air.

I quietly slip away while Ashton's back is turned, heading through the large kitchen to the decking out back. Kicking off my shoes, I walk barefoot toward the summer house at the bottom of the garden, enjoying the sensation of the cool grass beneath my feet.

I sit on the swing, shielded from the house by the ivy-covered trellis that wraps around one end of the small porch. This is my favorite place when I need some thinking space and a little peace and quiet. The combination of the wine and the fresh air has my head spinning, and I rest it against the swing. I'm almost dozing off when the sound of approaching footsteps warns me I'm about to have company.

"Thought I saw you sneak out," Brent says, appearing around the trellis. He sits on the swing next to me, sliding an arm along the back and around my shoulder.

"What are you doing?" I ask, looking pointedly at his hand resting on my shoulder and then back at him. He looks fuzzy, and I'm beginning to feel... peculiar. My head is heavy as if my neck can no longer support its weight.

"You okay? You look wasted," Brent replies, ignoring my question and narrowing his eyes on me.

I try to stand up, but the world sways around me, and bile crawls up my throat. "No. I don't feel well," I reply, my words slurred.

"Don't worry, baby. I'll take care of you," he purrs, his voice dropping suggestively as his arm tightens around my shoulders.

"I need to get back inside," I say, trying again to stand up. I groan, leaning forward as my stomach revolts at all the wine I've drunk.

"Why don't we go inside the summer house, and you can have a little lie down on the sofa," he says, helping me to my feet and urging me through the door.

Blackness creeps in around the edges of my vision, and I

stumble. A soft surface cushions my back as he lays me on the sofa.

"Did you think I wouldn't notice how you looked at Ashton?" Brent says next to my ear, and I crack my eyes open to see him looming over me. "He's the one, isn't he, Ivy? The reason I wasn't good enough? You want him, don't you? Got a thing for older men, eh? Hate to break it to you, but you don't stand a chance with a man like him. Tell you what, I'm gonna do you a favor and pop that cherry you've been guarding because no other fucker will be brave enough to fight their way through all that fat," he says nastily.

I want to hit him. I want to punch his teeth down his throat. But I can't seem to move. My body is heavy and sluggish.

"Fuck off, Brent," I sigh, letting my head flop back on the sofa.

It's a fight to keep my eyes open while nausea rolls in my stomach. There's a sudden tug at my chest, and cool air wafts across my skin. Brent has yanked my dress down, exposing my breasts.

His hands move to his belt buckle. "I usually like my women a little smaller, but I'm going to make an exception for you," he grunts, squeezing my breasts.

I try to push him away and open my mouth to yell at him to take his fucking hands off me, but my limbs are heavy, and I can't seem to form words. I want to sleep.

I hear a loud crash, and my eyes pop open momentarily. Brent is gone, and Ashton is standing over me, his face a mask of rage.

Then there's nothing.

# Chapter 4
# Ashton

I'm becoming more pissed off by the second, watching that asshole trail around after Ivy. Seems obvious to me all he wants is to get inside her panties.

*Isn't that what you want, too?* My conscience whispers.

I frown. No, that's not all I want. I'm not going to lie; having her lush curves beneath me while I fuck her raw has been an obsession of mine for years, but she's not a one-and-done deal for me. If I give in to the temptation that's been burning a hole in my gut for longer than I care to remember, I won't be able to walk away.

Rebecca, Kathy's friend, sidles up to me again, unloading episode twenty-four of 'Rebecca's Terrible Divorce' on my uninterested ears. A movement from the corner of my eye catches my attention, and I see a flushed Ivy making her way through the kitchen and out back. The urge to follow her is overwhelming. I know it's not a good idea, but I'm done with good ideas. I want to indulge in some very bad ideas. With Ivy.

I make my excuses to Rebecca and head for the back door, but another of Kathy's friends waylays me. I exchange polite pleasantries with the middle-aged woman for a moment until I see the guy who's been buzzing around Ivy all evening also heading outside.

Something about the way he checks over his shoulder before he slips out the door has my senses on red alert, but it takes me another few minutes to extricate myself from the conversation without raising suspicions unduly.

I step outside, following the path toward the summer house at the far end of the garden. Voices reach my ears as I approach.

"... I'm gonna do you a favor and pop that cherry you've been guarding because no other fucker will ever be brave enough to fight their way through all that fat!"

"Fuck off, Brent." Ivy's voice. She sounds... odd.

"I usually like my women a little smaller, but I'm going to make an exception for you."

*What the fuck?*

I round the trellis, and my blood turns to ice in my veins. Ivy is draped across the sofa in the summer house, her dress pulled down to expose her breasts, head lolling back drunkenly. The little fucker who's been following her around all night is looming over her, unzipping his fly.

I see red.

Pure, unadulterated rage engulfs me.

He doesn't stand a chance as I haul him away from her and my fist connects with his jaw. The punch sends him reeling into an occasional table behind him, but I'm not done yet. I fist my hand in the t-shirt at his throat and haul him up off the ground, only to deliver another blow to his slimy face. He slumps to the ground, out cold.

I turn to Ivy. Her eyes fix on me for a split second before they roll back in her head, and she passes out. I shrug off my jacket and cover her with it. My heart pounds as I realize what was about to happen here, what that shitbag was about to do to Ivy. *My* Ivy. He'll pay for that.

Things suddenly become crystal clear in my mind. I've been pushing her away for three years, but no more. I want her in my life. Under my roof, in my bed, in my arms.

I'm done waiting.

Two hours later, I'm back at my apartment with Ivy, who's still out cold.

How the fuck did I get myself into this position?

I've fought my feelings for this woman in my arms for three long years. I've worked through guilt, shame, and self-hatred, but it hasn't changed a goddammed thing. I want her. Pure and simple. Well, there's nothing pure about how I want her—it's more of a dark-edged obsession.

I wanted to kill the little fucker for what he tried to do, but I satisfied myself with messing his face up a little and calling the cops on his ass.

Kathy was beyond grateful I was there to stop the little shit. She was all for canceling her trip to New York tomorrow morning to defend her client in a high-profile court case, but I convinced her to let me bring Ivy home with me. It was the ideal solution. Kathy trusts me with her daughter.

But she shouldn't.

Because I'm casting my morals aside where Ivy is concerned. I'm selling my soul to the devil, and I can't bring myself to give a shit.

I place Ivy gently on my bed and strip her out of her torn dress. I'm tempted to slide her lace panties down her thighs too, but I'll save that little treat for later. The sight of her bare body almost brings me to my knees. She's thick and curvy, with large breasts, wide hips, and chunky thighs leading to a perfect little pussy with its neat strip of hair.

I drink in her luscious breasts tipped with their rosy crests. Her nipples are relaxed as she sleeps, and I want to see them harden for me, beg for my mouth like I want her to beg for my thick cock.

For the last three years, I haven't been able to come without thinking of her delectable body, without imagining sliding inside her tight, hot channel.

Tucking her under the sheet, I force myself to move away from her, feeling like a perverted voyeur. I head straight for the adjoining bathroom, stripping off my clothes as I go.

Once in the shower, I take myself in hand, the image of Ivy lying in my bed burned into my brain. I imagine I'm standing over her naked body, drops of my pre-cum falling onto her stomach as I fist myself over her in a punishing rhythm.

Harder and faster, I pound my swollen shaft, lost in my fantasies as the hot water cascades over me. I grit my teeth in frustration as I think about all the years I couldn't touch her, claim her. I come with a growl, imagining I'm shooting my cum all over her stomach and tits, marking her like a wild animal.

My orgasm barely takes the edge off. Thinking about her lying in my bed has my cock rock hard again.

I dress quietly so I don't disturb her, pulling on jeans and a t-shirt before heading for the living area.

My apartment is large, with an open-plan living, dining, and kitchen area. There are four bedrooms, all with adjoining bathrooms, a gym, a study, and a games room. Despite the size of the apartment, I don't do much entertaining here, preferring to keep my private and business lives separate.

The hugely successful construction company I've built from scratch has been my sole focus until the last few years. Then Ivy grew up, and my focus shifted. But her father, Jack, was my best friend. When he died of an unexpected heart attack at forty-two, I stepped in, becoming a shoulder for Kathy and a mentor for Ivy.

And that's where things became muddled. I didn't want to be her fucking mentor. I wanted to be the man in her life, in her bed. But things aren't muddled anymore. They're clearer than they've ever been.

I constantly check Ivy throughout the night and the following day, ensuring she's not sick. She barely stirs from the position I placed her in on the bed, and it's almost mid-afternoon the next day before she begins to stir.

It's time to explain that she's mine, and I'm not letting her go.

# Chapter 5
# Ivy

I crack my eyes open with a groan, vaguely aware that I'm naked except for my panties, my body covered by a single sheet. My head is pounding, and my mouth tastes like the inside of a sewer.

I move my head gingerly, trying to take in some of my surroundings. I'm lying in a strange bed, the mattress cocooning my body like a cloud of marshmallows.

I'm in a bedroom—a man's judging by the clothes folded neatly on the nearby chair and the items on the dresser.

"What the fuck?" I whisper to myself.

Where am I? And how did I get here? Have I been kidnapped?

The slamming of a door nearby makes me jump. I lie still, listening intently.

Should I call out? I shiver, exposed and vulnerable. Footsteps echo on hard flooring, and I hold my breath. Someone's coming. I pray whoever it is will keep walking. I need time to figure out where I am and get the hell out of here. The footsteps come to a halt outside the door. My breath is still trapped somewhere between my throat and my lungs.

*Think, Ivy! What's the last thing you remember?*

An image pops into my head as the door begins to open.

The last person I remember is... Ashton! Leaning over me after Brent tried to...

The door opens, and I close my eyes, trying to regulate my breathing. Hopefully, my kidnapper will think I'm still sleeping and leave me alone again.

My heart is beating a staccato against my ribs, and my chest rises and falls rapidly. I'm sure my kidnapper must be able to see the pulse beating at my throat.

"Don't panic, Ivy. You're safe," a deep voice murmurs.

I stiffen, and my eyes pop open along with my mouth. "Ashton?"

He frowns. He hates it when I use his full name, but I'm shocked to see him. No wonder I didn't recognize my surroundings—I've never been to his apartment.

"Yes, Ivy. It's Ash," he replies, stating the obvious.

My nipples harden beneath the thin sheet at the sound of his voice. His eyes drop, and I know he's clocked my body's betrayal by the tiny satisfied smile that pulls at his mouth.

"Why am I naked?" I demand. "How did I get here? What's going on?"

He moves to sit on the edge of the bed, reaching for the glass of water on the bedside table along with the ibuprofen he obviously placed there earlier. "Take these, and I'll explain."

I do as he asks, swallowing the pills and draining the glass.

He leans forward, smoothing his hand over my hair, watching with fascination as it sifts through his fingers. "Your friend, Brent, slipped a little something extra into your drink last night. He had every intention of forcing himself on you once it took hold," he explains, his face tight with anger.

I look at him in shock. "He—I—"

"Don't worry. I stopped him. Saw him follow you outside. God knows what the stupid fool thought he was doing, why he thought he'd get away with it. I took care of him, and your mom and I agreed you should come here while she's in New York. Your dress was ripped, so I stripped it off you. Then I left you to sleep off the drugs. I've been checking on you every hour or so since yesterday."

"Yesterday?" I look at him in disbelief. I pull myself into a sitting position, clutching the sheet to my chest. "How long was I out?

"Fifteen hours, give or take."

"Fifteen hours!" I squeak, trying to keep up.

He nods. "And one other thing. While you were sleeping in my bed, I jacked off in the shower, imagining I was fucking you raw."

My mouth drops open in shock as color runs up my neck and into my face. "I—I don't understand."

"You will. Soon," Ashton says, the deep timber of his voice sending shivers down my spine. "We have things we need to talk about, but I've waited too fucking long to get you naked in my bed. I won't wait any longer, Ivy."

Ashton moves suddenly, wrapping his hand around the sheet and slowly pulling it down my body. My eyes snap up to his, widening as I see the glittering intent in his gaze. This isn't a look I'm familiar with. His blue eyes darken to indigo, sending shivers down my spine and causing goosebumps to erupt across my breasts, tightening my nipples.

My fingers curl into the sheet at my breasts to stop him, but with one hard yank, he whips it away and tosses it onto the floor behind him. Instinctively, I wrap my arms around myself, trying to cover bountiful flesh with my hands. I know he won't hurt me, but the threat of his big body has desire and trepidation rushing through my bloodstream in equal amounts.

He drops one hand to my hip, squeezing my rounded flesh firmly enough to make me gasp. The sensation of his fingers biting into my skin sends a heated rush straight to my core, creating a pulse of need between my thighs.

Sweet Jesus, what is he doing to me? It's sinful. He's barely touched me, and I'm desperate to have him inside me. I think maybe I always have been.

Ashton's eyes drop to my lips as I run my tongue over them. It's like I can't help it. My body is taking over, tempting him, trying to lure him in. I want his kiss so badly, his tongue sliding against mine.

My eyes drink him in. His dark brown hair is now peppered with gray at the temples, but it only makes him even more attractive. Desire washes over me in a fierce wave. I can't breathe. I'm too hot.

He reaches out and runs a finger down my cheek, leaving a trail of fire in its wake. His head starts to dip towards me, and my breath freezes in my lungs.

Oh, God, he's going to give me what I want. He's going to kiss me.

His lips hover a scant inch from mine, but then he turns his head and buries his mouth against my throat. Wet warmth slides up my collarbone to my ear, blazing a trail of fire as he licks me like I'm his favorite dessert.

My whole being clenches as he catches my earlobe between his teeth and bites hard enough to cause a zing of pain. Lust hits me straight in my core. I can already feel my juices coating the tops of my thighs.

"You taste sweeter than anything I've ever had on my tongue," he rasps, his breath tickling my ear and making me shiver. "I know I've shocked you, but I'm done playing games. I'm hungry, Ivy, and you're the starter, main, and dessert."

My mouth opens, but the words get stuck in my throat. There's no mistaking his intentions. He wants me! I can see it in every line, every micro-expression on his face—a face that features in every one of my R-rated dreams. I hold my breath, wondering if those dreams are about to become a reality.

"You trust me, don't you, Ivy?" Ashton asks, his eyes boring into mine.

I tip my chin up. In for a penny... "I've always trusted you. Always wanted you."

He closes his eyes briefly, and when they open again, they're heavy with pleasure and... relief?

"Good, because you have no idea what the sight of you in my bed does to me. Fuck knows, I've waited a long time for this. I'm going to give you what you want, and I'm going to take what I need."

I'm beginning to get an idea of what he needs based on the intense look in his eyes. Does he feel the way I do? The idea has heat cascading through my body. The pulse between my legs intensifies, throbbing with my heartbeat, and I squeeze my thighs together to try to ease the ache.

"Yeah, you want it too, don't you, Kitten? I can tell by the way you're squeezing those luscious thighs together. Do you need me to ease the ache in that tight little pussy?"

I swallow hard, unable to find my voice, so I nod. His dirty words shock and thrill me simultaneously, and my body reacts viscerally, heart-pounding, nipples tightening. Am I still asleep? Have I slipped into one of my fantasies? Maybe I should pinch myself to see if this is real.

His breath escapes him in a hiss at my consent. His eyes drop to my body, sliding over me like a caress from the top of my head to the tips of my toes. "Perfect," he murmurs. "I love looking at your body. You gave me a glimpse in your bedroom that day, didn't you? Teasing me, showing me what I couldn't have."

He reaches out and moves my hands down to my sides. Leaning in closer, his mouth hovers an inch from mine. "I'm going to kiss you now, Ivy. And once I do, there's no going back. You'll be mine, understand?"

My breathing is labored as my eyes fix on his mouth. God, I want those lips on mine, taking me, claiming me, branding me his. "I understand."

He closes the remaining inch between us, brushing his mouth over mine before pulling back. I whimper, completely unsatisfied by that slight touch. I lift my hands, bunching them in his shirt. I lick my lips. "More," I demand.

Ashton slides his hands into my hair, pulling it tight in his fists and tilting my head back. "More, what?"

"More... please!" I choke at the mercy of my body.

"Better," he nods.

His mouth hits mine, and I moan in pleasure. He uses the opening to thrust his tongue inside my mouth, sliding it against mine. The kiss is rough and desperate, fueled by years of want and lust. Everything about this is forbidden, naughty—and so very right.

I kiss him back ferociously, wriggling closer so I'm practically in his lap, grinding myself against him. One powerful thigh sits between my legs, and I give in to the temptation to rub myself against him. It's incredible and electrifying, and my clit throbs as heat builds deep in my core.

"You trying to make me cum in my pants, Kitten? I'd rather cum all over your face and tits, mark you with my seed," he rasps, his hands tightening almost painfully on my hips.

He flips me onto my back with one deft movement, so I'm sprawled in the middle of the bed, completely at his mercy.

"Please!" I beg, unconsciously arching my body.

"Don't worry, Ivy. I'm going to take care of you. Lie still and let me look at you."

He slides his hands along my thighs and yanks my panties down my legs. Slowly, he spreads my thighs open, adjusting his position so he's right between them. He runs his index finger along the seam of my pussy, making me moan.

"God, you're so fucking wet for me," he growls. "You smell like fresh apples and sin. I need to clean you up, baby, lick you clean."

Dear God, this is too much! My body is burning up in a ball of fire.

"You want that, don't you, Ivy? For me to take care of this wet little cunt?" he asks, drawing tantalizing circles around my swollen lips.

I squeeze my eyes shut, trying to process my body's needs. Something powerful is building inside me. I've masturbated numerous times with his image in my head, but it's never felt like this before—and he's barely touched me.

Ashton shifts his weight, sliding his body up mine. His chest presses against my hard nipples, the delicious abrasion of his shirt reminding me he's still fully dressed.

"Open your eyes," he demands, rocking his hips against mine.

My eyes fly open on a moan, and I bite my lip hard at the sensations crowding my core.

"Ask me, Ivy."

"Ask—ask you what?"

"Ask me to lick your pussy clean."

Oh, sweet heavenly lord, he's undoing me with his words. "Ashton, p-please lick me clean."

He frowns. "Try again, Kitten. You know I don't like it when you call me Ashton."

I do as he asks, beyond caring now. I need him to quench the ache in my body. "Ash, please lick my pussy clean."

He smiles in satisfaction before he pulls away from me. My hands reach for him automatically, trying to yank him back, but he moves out of my reach. He kneels between my thighs and pulls his shirt from his jeans, unbuckling his belt and sliding it free.

"Unbutton me," he orders.

I move closer, doing as he asks and popping the buttons

open one by one. He's not wearing underwear and his thick cock springs from its confines.

"Wrap your hand around it, Kitten. Feel what you do to me. What you've done to me since you were sixteen years old."

My eyes fly to his, stunned at his confession. "Since I was sixteen? But—"

"Yeah, I know I'm a sick fucker. I'm eighteen years older than you. You're the daughter of my best friend. When I promised your father I'd look after you, I'm pretty fucking sure he didn't mean this. But it doesn't matter because I can't fight it anymore. I want you more than I want my next breath."

I sense the shift of power—he's made himself vulnerable to me. I don't know what to say, but it's okay. Actions speak louder than words. Isn't that what they say?

I move so I'm kneeling in front of him. I lean in, and my mouth settles over his as my hands wrap around his cock. He hisses and jerks as I slide my thumb over the fluid at its tip, rubbing it in circles around the head. I break the kiss, bringing my thumb to my mouth to taste him. I make a humming noise as I suck it clean. "You taste amazing."

Ash growls and pushes me back down on the bed so I'm flat on my back again. He takes his cock in his hand and rubs it against my pussy, coating himself in my juices.

"You like the way I taste? Do you want more? You want my cum smeared across your lips, filling up this tight cunt?" he rasps, guiding his cock against my sex so it bumps my clit.

I'm incapable of answering, so I moan, thrashing my head on the pillow. The sounds spilling from my throat are shocking, but I can't contain them.

"Yeah, you like that, don't you? Let me hear how much you like what I'm doing to your pussy, Ivy!"

I whimper and moan as he slides the tip of his cock along my wet cleft, hitting the small bundle of nerves with each pass.

"No one else touches this pussy, Ivy. It belongs to me, and I'm going to be inside it every chance I get from now on. I'm going to claim every one of your tight little holes, show you what it's like to come with my cock inside you."

That's all it takes to send me over the edge. My body spasms, and my back arches off the bed. Sensations heap one on top of another as I come hard. He flicks his cock against my clit again and again as I ride the wave. I hear him grunt, and warm liquid splashes against my skin as he finds his release.

I open my eyes to find Ash gazing down at me, a smile tugging at his mouth. "We've made a fine mess of your pussy now, haven't we, Kitten?"

Color hits my cheeks, and I lift my hands to cover my embarrassment.

He grips my hands, easing them back down. "Don't hide from me. Not anymore," he rumbles, leaning forward to run his nose along my cheek.

His lips trail down, and I arch my neck to give him better access. He feathers them across my collarbones and over the swell of my tits. His mouth hovers over the rosy crest of one, his tongue darting out to tease the nub.

"Oh, God!" I cry out at the subtle caress, marveling at how easily and completely this man turns me on. He's hypnotizing me with touch, his smell, his lips, and I never want to wake from his spell.

Then, he's feasting on them, scooping them up in his hands and nipping and sucking at my nipples. I gasp and squirm as his hand moves between us, and he uses his fingers to smear our combined juices around my clit. It's so fucking dirty, yet incredibly hot.

He moves down my body, nipping and licking at every inch of skin before settling his head between my thighs again. Surely, he's not going to...?

His mouth settles over my mound, and he takes one long swipe across my cleft with his tongue. The warm wetness mixing with our fluids is beyond heavenly. He slides his hands beneath my butt, holding me still while his mouth ravages me. He licks and sucks at my pussy like he's French kissing my mouth. My God, this man is not shy about going down on me!

I thrash beneath him despite the firm grip of his fingers on my hips, but it only makes him lock his mouth onto me harder, a growl erupting from his throat.

"Holy fuck!" I pant as he circles my clit with the tip of his tongue.

He pulls back a little to look at me, a gleam of satisfaction in his blue eyes. "I've got you, Kitten. Spread yourself wider for me, and let me see what's mine. I want every drop of cream that gushes from this cunt."

He takes my hand and guides it to my pussy, and I use my fingers to hold my swollen lips open for him. He hums in appreciation, latching his mouth onto me again and dragging his tongue back and forth in a maddening rhythm.

"Please, Ash!" I plead, not sure how much more I can take.

He lifts his head briefly, and I look down at him. "Hold tight, baby."

He dips his head again, sucking hard at my clit, and my orgasm blows through me in an explosion of bliss. I hear myself scream as I ride the wave, shaking and shivering as I slowly come back down.

I'm vaguely aware of his weight shifting off the bed, and I open my mouth to protest. Is he leaving me? I don't think I can bear for things to go back to how they were after this. He already had my heart, but now he also has my body and soul.

Then I hear the shower running, and seconds later, he's back, scooping me up in his arms. "My dirty girl needs to get clean," he says, striding towards the adjoining bathroom.

He lowers me into the huge shower cubicle, stripping off the rest of his clothes before joining me. His hand immediately slides between my legs, cupping me in his palm. "This is mine now."

I lick my lips and nod. I'm not arguing. It's been his for a while.

He brushes my hair back from my face with a tender hand, studying my face. "What's wrong, Ivy? Didn't you like what we did?"

I drop my eyes from his penetrating gaze. Maybe I imagined the words he whispered and the desire I saw in his eyes. He's behind every one of my fantasies, and they're sending me a little crazy. I've imagined scenarios like this so many times while I touched myself that I'm sure I'm caught up in another.

"I loved it, but I'm trying to keep up. You've barely looked at me lately. I've missed you, but—I'm not sure what this is," I say, waving a hand between us.

"It's what it was always meant to be. I'm not going anywhere, Kitten, and I'm sure as fuck not letting you go. I meant what I said earlier. You're mine. Every delectable curve and dimple, every inch of skin. All mine."

His words reassure me. I'm a grown woman. I should hate his possessive talk, but I don't. I crave it like I crave him.

Grabbing the shower gel and a soft washcloth, he gently washes my body. Then he squeezes some shampoo into his palm and massages it through my scalp. I sigh blissfully, losing myself in the sensation of being cared for. Cherished.

*Loved?*

Once he's rinsed my hair clean, he tugs me out of the shower and carries me back to the bedroom, setting me down on the edge of the bed. I love how he seems to move me around at his will. He makes me feel feminine and nurtured.

"Scoot your butt to the edge, lean back and open your legs for me," he instructs.

I shiver with anticipation, doing as he says. I rest my weight on my elbows cland bend my knees, completely opening myself up to him.

He moves between my legs and lowers himself to his knees so his face is level with my pussy. He slides a finger along my puffy lips, and my hips rise instinctively, seeking a deeper contact.

His eyes cut to mine. "Now, I'm going to eat you. And then, if you're a good girl, I'm going to fuck you."

# Chapter 6
# Ashton

I spread Ivy's legs wider, opening her sweet pussy to me. Her breasts are heavy—two delectable mounds that jiggle as she shifts on the mattress. They taunt me with their perfection. Licking my lips, I can still taste a trace of our mixed juices in my mouth from earlier. Instantly I'm hard, a drizzle of pre-cum leaking from the tip of my cock.

I've had women, but I've never been at the mercy of one like I am with Ivy. She may not know it yet, but I'm as vulnerable to her as she is to me. And it's not only sexual. For years, I've watched her, known her, first as a protector and mentor and then as the woman she's become. Beautiful. Strong. Feisty. Sexy as hell.

She hasn't experienced all the world has to offer yet, but she's going to—with me. My desire for her is edged with darkness, but while I may want to dominate her in the bedroom, she'll soon learn she can bring me to my knees everywhere else.

I've allowed my own selfish needs to drive me to this point, this situation. But I don't regret it. I'll give Ivy whatever she wants, whenever she wants it, so long as she's by my side. She'll only ever need me, my mouth on her, my cock inside her as she begs me for release. I plan on being inside her tight cunt or her pink asshole at every opportunity, so she may as well start getting used to it right now.

"You are exquisite," I breathe, running my eyes over her naked body before settling my gaze between her legs.

Her cheeks flush at the compliment, and she bites her lip uncertainly. I can see she doubts my words, and my heart squeezes in my chest.

"Look at me," I command, tearing my eyes from my prize and focusing on her face. "I'll never lie to you, Ivy. You're the most beautiful woman I've ever laid eyes on, and I'm damned lucky to be the one who gets to touch you like this. I don't care what that stupid fucking kid told you. You're everything I've ever wanted, ever dreamed of, in a woman. Never forget that."

Her face lights up at my words, and her eyes glisten with unshed tears. "Ash," she whispers, moved by my words.

She looks so fucking gorgeous like this, with her blond hair curling damply around her shoulders, her pink skin, and her honey-brown eyes. She smiles at me like

I'm her manna from heaven, and my ego does a tap dance.

My eyes drop back between her thighs. "I need another taste. I need your pussy scent all over my face."

"Oh, God, you say the dirtiest things," Ivy moans.

"And you love it!"

"I do," she whispers, her eyes heavy with desire.

I push her thighs further apart, and she lifts her hips an inch. She knows how good this will be, how good I'm going to make her feel because I'm the one in control of her pleasure.

"Push that pussy into my mouth, Kitten. Show me how much you want my lips and my tongue."

She shivers and spreads her legs wider, thrusting her cunt closer to my face. I grunt with satisfaction as I see how wet she is for me, how needy.

I run my hands over her meaty thighs and around her stomach. She's curvy and voluptuous everywhere, with acres of skin I can't get enough of. My hands find her tits, and I pinch her nipples between my fingers as I settle my mouth over the puffy, pink lips of her pussy.

Ivy groans and rolls her hips rhythmically against me, trying to get off against my mouth. I draw one whole lip into my mouth and suckle it before doing the same to the other. Her cream overflows from her pussy and runs down her cleft towards her ass. I dive in, licking it up like a wild animal slathering at its only source of nourishment. Because she *is* my nourishment. She's the air I breathe and the reason I get out of bed in the morning.

My hands continue to squeeze and massage her heavy tits while I lap and suckle at her clit. I'm tempted to slide a finger or two inside her, but I want my cock to be the first thing inside her tight channel. Her inner walls will be molded to the shape of my cock, because it's the only one she'll have inside her.

My control begins to slip as I continue to eat her, sipping up the juices oozing around her inner thighs. She fists her hands in my hair as I rub my face against her pussy like a cat, coating my face in her. Every time my stubble abrades her sensitive flesh, she jerks and gasps, twitching against me like she's being tortured.

I grab her leg and throw it over my shoulder while I go to town on her. She shifts her hips forward, and my hands go to her ass, spreading her cheeks open so my tongue can find her tight, pink hole. I run my tongue along her, back and forth, while my thumb finds her clit and presses firmly.

"Ash!" she mewls as the tip of my tongue presses inside her tight ass. She keeps moaning my name over and over again as I pleasure her. The noises she's making as I lick her asshole have me teetering on the edge.

"Ash, I'm going to—" Her face screws up, and her thighs squeeze my head as she grinds herself against my face. She gushes into my mouth, her cries echoing around the bedroom, and that's all it takes for me to find my release.

I cum all over myself, my cock pulsing streams down my thighs. Her cunt sucks at my face, her thighs gripping me while she rides out her climax until, eventually, her shivers stop, and she slumps back onto the bed.

I lower her leg from my shoulder and push myself to my feet on shaking legs. Ivy looks at me, her eyes half-mast with the echoes of her pleasure. They slide down my body, widening as she sees my cum drizzled across my thighs.

She licks her lips. "Did you...?"

"Cum all over myself? Yeah, that's what you do to me," I say sheepishly, leaning into her and claiming her mouth in a quick kiss.

She looks inordinately pleased with herself, her mouth curved in a soft smile, her eyes running over me hungrily. I'm not ripped with muscle, but I'm fit and healthy and keep in shape. If the way her tongue darts out to wet her lips as she looks at me is any indication, she likes what she sees. The weight of her eyes on me has my cock rock hard again.

Jesus, this woman!

My cock is going to have to wait a little longer. I plan to take my time with Ivy and make a banquet of her—but first, I need to feed her. Then, I'll fuck her.

"Enjoying the view?" I ask with a smirk, turning to face her.

"I want to touch you. Taste you," she says, looking at my turgid shaft with its bead of pre-cum glistening on the end. "You're still hard, but... you came twice," she says, confused.

Tell me about it. I don't think my dick has gone down since he decided there was only one pussy he's interested in. "It's always like this around you, Ivy. He won't go down until he gets inside you, and even then, he won't stay down for long."

Ivy trails her fingers over her magnificent tits, circling her nipples. "So? What are you waiting for?"

I prowl toward her, my shaft bobbing in front of me. "If you want it, you need to ask nicely, Kitten."

"Ash, I want your cock inside me," she says immediately. Her hips undulate as she says it, and I'm willing to bet my left nutsack she's wet for me again. I can practically smell her arousal.

I sigh. "Where are your manners?"

"Please," she whispers, her eyes needy.

I lean down, caging her in with my arms. "Don't worry, baby. I'm going to stuff you full of my cock soon enough. By the time I'm done with you, there won't be an inch of skin left unmarked by my mouth or my cum, but first of all, I'm going to feed you."

I move away from her, going commando as I pull on a pair of sweatpants. If I'm going to spend the next few hours with an erection, I need to give it a little freedom. Plus, she'll see how much I want her, how hard I am for her. Constantly.

I grab one of my t-shirts for her, pulling her to her feet and sliding it over her head. It lands below her rounded butt. Perfect. Tantalizing. There's nothing sexier than seeing her in one of my shirts. I take her hand and thread our fingers together, smiling as I lead her from the bedroom to the kitchen.

I throw some sandwiches and a salad together while she perches on one of the bar stools, her eyes glued to me as I move around the kitchen. She's quiet, and I know she has questions burning on the tip of her tongue.

I place her food in front of her and pull up a stool opposite. "You eat. I'll talk," I say, nodding with satisfaction as she picks up her ham sandwich and takes a bite. "Do you know why I brought you here, Ivy?"

She swallows her mouthful before answering. "Because Brent tried to rape me, and Mom didn't want to leave me in the house alone."

I study her closely. It's clear she still believes that, despite what we've shared up to this point. "That's only a small part of it. I told you earlier that I've wanted you for years, a fact I've wrestled with time and time again. I've watched you grow into a beautiful woman who's stolen my heart to the point where I haven't been with anyone else for years. You're the only one I want, Ivy, from now to the grave."

I take a deep breath, forcing myself to continue. She needs to know it all so she can make her decision. "I want all of you. I want to share everything with you, show you different places, and cheer you on in your career. I want to be the man in your life, put a ring on your finger, and plant my seed in your womb. You told me you want me, but if you don't want me in the same way, this is your only chance to leave. Because once I get inside you, I'll tie you to the fucking bed to keep you."

Her eyes widen as I finish. Her sandwich lies forgotten on her plate. She's silent for so long, it scares me. After a minute, she stands, moving toward me and pressing my legs open on the stool so she can settle her hips between them.

"You don't need to tie me to the bed to keep me, Ash," she murmurs, threading her hands through my hair. "I've been yours since before I was legal, in here," she says, placing a hand over her heart.

That's all I need to hear. I scoop Ivy up and head for the bedroom.

# Chapter 7
# Ivy

Ash yanks back the sheet and tosses me onto the bed. I giggle as I pull my t-shirt over my head, watching as he divests himself of his sweatpants. He crawls onto the bed next to me, caging me with his big body.

"I'm clean, Kitten, but I'll use something if you want," he says.

I love that he's getting the practicalities out of the way before he fucks me senseless. "I'm on the pill," I reply with a smile. "I want you bare."

"Fuck, I was hoping you were going to say that," he rasps.

It almost broke me to hear him tell me how much he wanted me and for how long. All those wasted years when we could've been together. But he was trying to do the right thing, and I love him all the more for it.

He thinks his morals are questionable because of his feelings for me, but I know better. He wants to be mine, and I want to be his. I want everything he wants.

And right now, he wants me desperately, judging by the way his hard cock is nudging at my stomach. I haven't had a chance to fulfill one of my fantasies with him yet—but I'm about to.

I push him so he rolls onto his back. Running my hands down his hard stomach, I follow the happy trail of hair down his abs to his hard cock. He hisses as I grab it with one hand, sliding it up and down with firm strokes.

"Ivy," he grunts, his voice rough with passion.

Yeah. Pretty sure he likes that.

I give him a few more pumps, and he releases a groan. He reaches for my hand, wrapping his own around it and squeezing hard. I'm working on instinct, fisting this weapon of mass destruction, but I guess Ash likes it firmer, rougher.

I continue to squeeze and pump, flushed with pleasure as Ash's breathing picks up. He grunts and groans, thrusting his hips in rhythm with my hand. Now I know what he likes, he removes his hand, letting me fly solo.

"That's it, Kitten. Work my cock like you own it," he gasps.

I can't believe how turned on I am by his responses. It's amazing, knowing I'm responsible for his pleasure.

I speed up my movements, seeing a bead of moisture leak from the end. Holding him firm, I dip my head, flicking my tongue along his slit to swipe it up. I hum as the taste of him explodes on my tongue. I open my mouth around him, taking him deep inside and circling my tongue around the head.

"Deeper," he demands roughly. "Take me all the way in."

I relax my throat until his tip hits the back, fighting my gag reflex. He's big and thick, and I'm struggling to fit him all in, but I'm not giving up. I suck him harder, faster, reveling in the noises coming from his throat. I'm so turned on that my juices ooze down my inner thighs.

"I'm going to come, Kitten, and you're going to swallow every last drop," he rasps, his hands moving to my head, digging into my scalp as I continue to deep-throat him.

"Holy fucking shit!" he roars, spilling his hot seed down my throat.

I do as he says and swallow every last bit, licking him clean as the last of his orgasm ebbs away. Amazingly, impossibly, he's still hard, and I lift bemused eyes to his.

"I told you he's not going down until I get inside you," he reminds me with an arrogant smirk.

Well, fuck. He wasn't lying.

I slide up his body, and he pulls my head down to his for a deep kiss, sliding his tongue inside my mouth in long, slow strokes. Without breaking the kiss, he flips me onto my back, settling his weight on his elbows. His dick presses against my stomach. Holy crap, it's harder than ever. This man is a fucking sex god.

He breaks the kiss, staring down at me as he sweeps my damp hair away from my face. "I'm going to take you now, Kitten. Make you mine."

His words are a promise, and I shiver in anticipation. "You ruined me for anyone else, you know that, right? You'll be my first and my last."

Ash swallows hard, his eyes full of emotion. "I know, Kitten. You saved herself for me, didn't you? Makes me humble. But it also makes me want to roar and beat my chest like a fucking caveman."

"Make me yours, Ash. And do it like you mean it," I demand, holding his intense blue gaze.

He smiles and swoops in for another kiss while he lines his cock up with my entrance, barely penetrating me. He slides it along my cleft a few times, wetting it with my juices. And then he thrusts in deep.

"Holy shit!" I shout, my eyes rolling back in my head as I lose all the breath in my lungs. It hurts, but the pain is fleeting. Nothing has ever felt as good as being filled by the man I love.

"Fuck, Ivy! You're so fucking tight!" Ash grunts, forcing himself to hold still while I adjust to his length and girth.

He still hasn't moved after several seconds. "If you don't move soon, I'm going to scream," I rasp, wrapping my legs around his hips and digging my heels into his ass.

He groans and pulls back a few inches before plunging inside me again. I cry out in pleasure, dropping my eyes to watch as his thick cock disappears inside me again and then again. It's the most erotic thing I've ever seen, and I'm already teetering on the verge of an orgasm. I struggle to draw in air and not come all at once as he thrusts back in, even deeper this time.

He grabs my legs and hooks them over his shoulders right before he ruts into me with a force and depth that has me screaming his name. My pussy grips him greedily as he pounds into me, pain mixing with pleasure at his forceful rhythm. The position of our bodies allows him to go so deep that I swear the tip of him is touching my womb.

"God, I love being inside you! You're so fucking tight. Your cunt has my cock in a death grip," he grunts above me, his hips moving like pistons as he fucks me hard.

I mewl at his dirty words of encouragement. As he said earlier, I'm finally getting what I want, what we both need. My hips move frantically beneath him, matching him thrust for thrust. An orgasm is building in my core that I'm pretty sure is going to wreck me.

"I'm close!" I sob, gripping his shoulders tightly to brace myself as he almost fucks me off the end of the bed.

He leans down and pulls a nipple into his mouth, sucking on it hard, and I fly over the edge, shouting my ecstasy into the room. His shout joins mine as my pussy clamps down on him, milking his orgasm from him. A layer of sweat slicks our bodies as he plows into me, filling me to the brim with every drop of his cum until it spills out between us.

Finally, with one last groan, he pushes into me as far as he can go and then collapses on top of me. I lower my legs from his shoulders, my pussy still holding his cock tightly. Slowly, we come back down to earth, our breathing harsh in the quiet of the room. My body is flushed, still stuffed full of his cock, electrified with little aftershocks from the hardest climax I've ever experienced.

I peek up at Ash with a satisfied smile, and the way he's looking at me takes my breath away. Like I'm his queen. He kisses me, slow and deep and tender, bringing a lump to my throat.

"Are you okay, Kitten?" he asks in concern.

"Better than okay. Amazing," I whisper.

"No words," he mutters, his expression stunned. "I have no words to describe what we just shared."

"I do," I murmur. "It's love. I love you, Ash. Always have. Always will."

He dips his head to mine again, kissing me as if he'll never get enough of my mouth. "I love you, too, Ivy."

He lifts his weight off me, and we both groan as he slips out of me. He's still semi-hard, despite coming twice in the last hour. It's a heady sensation, knowing we get to do this again and again.

He pulls me into him, arranging me so he's spooning me from behind, his hand cupping my breast. I snuggle back against him, completely content, and his dick slides between my ass cheeks, the head nudging my sensitive clit.

"Dear God, does it ever go down?" I ask in wonder.

His laugh is a rumble against my back. "I did warn you. He's been hard for you for years, Kitten. But you're mine now, and I plan to get inside your pretty little pussy as often as is humanly possible."

"Sounds good," I mumble, my eyelids drooping.

He presses a kiss on my shoulder. "Sleep now."

I close my eyes with a sigh. I finally have everything I've ever wanted. I hope I can hold onto him.

# Chapter 8
## Ashton

I wake up the following day with Ivy draped across my body. Gently disentangling myself without waking her, I get up and head for the bathroom to wash up.

There's something I need to do, and it's better if I do it alone.

An hour later, I'm knocking on Kathy's door, having called ahead to tell her I was on my way. She opens the front door with a welcoming smile. "Ash! Good to see you." Her eyes move past me, looking for Ivy. She returned from New York late last night, and I know she's expecting me to return with her daughter. "Where's Ivy?"

"Can I come in?" I ask instead of answering her question.

"Of course." She moves back, holding the door open for me, and I step inside, watching as she closes it behind me. "Is everything okay? Is Ivy okay? I tried to call last night to see how she was, but there was no reply from either of your cells."

"She's fine," I'm quick to reassure her. "She was tired, so I left her sleeping."

A slight frown puckers Kathy's brow at my choice of words, but it's quickly gone as she turns towards the living room. She has no reason not to trust me. There's no way she'd suspect I took her daughter's virginity and fucked her raw last night.

"How was your trip?" I ask, following her through to the lounge.

"All good so far. It's preliminaries right now. I fly back the day after tomorrow. This case will go on for a while," she replies, taking a seat on the expensive leather sofa.

I sink down in the chair opposite her. No expense has been spared on the décor of this house or Ivy's education. Kathy earns good money as a defense lawyer and has given her daughter every advantage without turning her into a spoiled brat. She loves her as much as I do.

Which is why this is going to be so hard.

"So, Ivy's okay? I was so worried about her after what happened with Brent. I'm grateful to you for stepping in to help, Ash. What on earth did that stupid boy think he was doing, putting his hands on my daughter? He won't get away with it. I'll see he doesn't," Kathy seethes.

"I know you will," I say solemnly, understanding how protective she is of Ivy. I get it. On the one hand, she wants her to be independent, but on the other, she doesn't want to lose her little girl. "But there is something I need to tell you. About Ivy."

Kathy's eyes narrow on me, concern in their depths. "You said she was okay."

"She is," I quickly reassure her. "She doesn't know I'm here, but I thought I should be the one to tell you."

"Tell me what?"

"I love Ivy."

She laughs. "I know you do, Ash. You've been like a father to her since Jack died. I don't know what we would've done without you."

I wince at her words. "I don't love her like a father, Kathy. I love her like a man loves a woman he wants to spend the rest of his life with. I love her for the woman she's become."

Kathy stares at me. When she speaks again, her voice is deadly calm, and I get a glimpse of what she must be like in the courtroom. "Are you trying to tell me you're sleeping with my daughter?"

I meet her accusing gaze without flinching. "Kathy, please let me explain everything before you jump to conclusions."

Her mouth tightens, but she gives me the smallest of nods. I release the breath I was holding, grateful she hasn't immediately ripped my balls off and fed them to me.

"I know I've blindsided you, but this isn't a sudden development for me. Or for Ivy. It's why I haven't been around so much lately. Being near her was torture. My feelings for her started to change three years ago, hell, maybe even before," I admit, deciding to lay it all on the table. "But I never acted on anything before last night. At first, I thought I needed a little space to sort my head out, but it didn't change my feelings for her. If anything, they've grown stronger."

I pause, running a hand over my face as I try to put everything into words.

"Honestly, these last three years, I thought I was losing it. I've tried so fucking hard to fight what I feel for her, but I can't do it anymore. You know me, Kathy. You know the life I live. I'm not some creepy predator looking for my next conquest. I've waited my whole life for her. I love her more than anything else in this world. I want to make her happy. And what makes her happy is me. So, the way I see it, we can fight about this and ruin our friendship, or you can accept we're going to be together for the long haul. And if you can't accept it, if this means the end of our friendship, I want you to know Ivy and I will be together regardless. I'll always love and protect her because she's my number one priority."

Kathy's face doesn't show any emotion once I've finished my outburst. Her poker face is another skill that makes her a great defense lawyer. It seems like forever until she finally releases a breath and leans back on the sofa.

"This isn't all about you and what you want, Ash. What about Ivy's future?" she asks, beginning the cross-examination.

"Being with me won't affect her future. If anything, I can take her places and show her things she wouldn't get to see otherwise. You know my financial situation. I'm obscenely rich and have more money than I can spend in a single lifetime, courtesy of my construction businesses here in Houston. Now, I'll spend some of that money on her, doing whatever she wants. If she wants a career, fine, I'm all in. If she wants to travel and see the world, that works, too. But whichever way you look at it, whatever we do, we'll be doing it together because I can't live without her, and I know she feels the same."

Kathy falls quiet again, stretching my nerves to their limit. Ivy is very much like her mom. She's going to keep me on my toes, and I can't fucking wait.

"I don't need the details, but you said you weren't intimate until last night?" she finally asks.

I nod, holding her gaze so she can see the truth of my words. "I would never take advantage of Ivy. She wanted me as much as I wanted her."

Kathy purses her lips thoughtfully. "She's my daughter, and I love her very much, but it seems she's always craved a life different from most. She's got a maturity most women her age don't possess, which is why I'm confident she knows what she wants. I know I've sheltered her to some extent, particularly since Jack died, but I would never stop her from walking her own path in life. And if that path includes you, then I won't stand in the way."

She pauses, the eyes so like her daughter's boring into me. "But am I happy about it? No. The age gap worries me, but only time will tell if you mean what you say. We have a friendship I value greatly, and I know it will hurt Ivy if one of us isn't a part of her life. So I'll trust you with my daughter's heart, but know that if you ever break it, our friendship will be over."

I admire her ferocity for her daughter because it's the same ferocity I have for Ivy.

I smile. "That's not going to happen. So I guess you're stuck with me."

# Chapter 9
# Ivy

I wake to find the space next to me empty. I yawn and stretch, my muscles sore in the best way. Last night was... everything. All my hopes and dreams rolled up into one big, growly man who seems to want me and love me as much as I love him.

A door slams nearby. I jump and then become still, listening intently. I hear footsteps. Someone is coming. I hold my breath, praying it's Ash. It's like a re-run of yesterday morning, only this time, I know exactly where I am and why I'm naked.

The bedroom door opens, and Ash stands there, dressed in a button-down shirt and suit pants. He looks edible.

"Morning, beautiful," he says, removing items of clothing as he stalks towards the bed.

"Where do you think you've been?" I ask with a pout. "I woke up, and you weren't here."

"Don't worry, Kitten. I won't ever be away from your side for long," he says, sliding his boxers down his legs so his hard cock bounces free.

I lick my lips. "You didn't answer my question," I say, trying to focus as he climbs into bed next to me, pulling me flush with his hard body.

"I went to see your mom."

I pull back to look at him. "*What?*"

He tells me everything while he smooths his hands over my skin, through my hair, as if he can't stop touching me.

"So... she was okay? About us?" I ask in disbelief. I'm unsure whether I'm angry or grateful he went to see Mom without me. I'll decide later after I've punished him a little with my mouth.

"As fine as she's going to be until she sees we're not playing around," he replies. "I think she took it pretty fucking well under the circumstances. I thought she was going to serve my balls up to me on a platter."

"Yeah, she's more than capable of doing something like that when it comes to her loved ones," I say with a wry smile.

Mom loves ferociously, which is why she's never pursued a relationship with anyone else since Dad died. She'll come to see that Ash and I love each other as ferociously as she and Dad did.

"So, what now?" I ask, sliding my hand down his firm abs and grasping his hard cock.

He hisses through his teeth, but to my surprise, he gently disentangles himself from me and gets up. I gaze at his broad shoulders and muscled ass as he crosses to a chest of drawers, wondering what he's up to. He opens the top one and removes something before turning and walking back towards the bed.

Perching on the edge, he opens the small velvet box in his hand a removes a beautiful solitaire diamond ring. He reaches for my left hand, sliding it onto my ring finger and nodding with approval when it fits perfectly.

"I've been waiting to put that ring on your finger for three years," he says, lifting my hand to his mouth and kissing my knuckles.

My mouth drops open, and I gape at him, speechless. "Does that mean—are you asking me to marry you?"

He shakes his head. "Not asking. Telling."

Warmth floods my girlie bits at his no-nonsense reply. "Then I guess you should know you have no choice either. I'm marrying you whether you want to or not."

He laughs at my display of defiance. "Never in doubt, Kitten, never in doubt."

I nod. "Good to know we're on the same page."

He pushes me back on the bed, looming over me. "Oh, we're on the same page. Of the same book. In the same library."

I giggle at his words, cupping his face in my hands. "I love you, Ash."

He dips his head, claiming a kiss. "I love you too, Ivy."

"Then show me."

He understands what I need. "Does someone's pussy need a little attention?" he asks, inserting his thigh between my legs.

I rub myself against it shamelessly, biting my lip as wet heat pools between my legs. "I need you so badly it hurts."

"I'm going to take care of you," he promises, sliding his hand between my legs and pulling my pussy lips open so he can circle my clit. He keeps the pressure where I need it while he slides his thumb backward, pushing it into my asshole. The combination of his finger on my clit and his thumb in my ass has me mewling uncontrollably.

"Yeah, you like that, don't you, Kitten? You like my thumb inside that tight, pink hole. I'm loosening you up, sweet girl, because I'll be stuffing it full of my cock before long."

"Oh, God!" I choke, my insides liquefying with my approaching climax.

"That's it, Ivy, get yourself off on my hand," he encourages, bending to suckle at my nipples.

I hear a keening sound and realize it's me as I come so hard that I almost blackout. Before I have a chance to recover, he plunges inside me with one powerful thrust.

"Ohgodohgodohgod!" I chant, pulling my knees up by his hips so he can go deeper, harder.

His mouth attacks my body, grazing his teeth along my neck and biting at my nipples as he ruts against me like a wild animal. And I love it, love every hard, rough thrust of his hips against mine.

He rolls us over so I'm straddling him, and his hands drop to my hips. "I want you to ride me. I want to watch your tits bounce as you get yourself off on my cock," he demands, reaching up to pluck at my nipples.

No need to ask me twice. I undulate my hips, lifting off him before sinking down again. My head lolls back on my shoulders as I move my hips, surging against him and taking him deep.

"That's it, Kitten. Ride me hard. God, you're so fucking incredible, every inch of you."

His words spur me on, and I ride him harder and faster, working us both toward a release of epic proportions.

"I'm close! So, so close!" I gasp, my internal muscles tightening with the onslaught of another orgasm.

Ash rises, wrapping an arm around me as he pistons his hips. Our bodies come together with wet slaps as his balls bounce off my ass cheeks. His other hand spears into my hair, pulling me down for his kiss, and I scream my climax into his mouth, squirting my juices all over his thighs.

He grunts and spasms and then becomes still as he unloads himself inside me with one final shout of ecstasy.

Slowly, slowly, I come back down to earth, slumped and spent, my body draped over his.

"Ash?"

"Yeah?"

"Can we stay like this forever?"

I can hear the smile in his voice as he replies, "Forever is a long time, Kitten."

I lift my head, resting my chin on his chest as I look up at him, seeing all my love for him reflected in his eyes. "Not nearly long enough.

# Epilogue 1
## Ashton

It's time. I've claimed my woman in every sense of the word apart from the official one. I'm an old-fashioned fucker, and I want the piece of paper saying she's mine and I'm hers.

It's just Kathy, Ivy, and me at the registry office. Ivy didn't want an extravagant ceremony. She wants me however she can get me—words she uttered two nights ago as I buried my face in her sweet pussy until she screamed my name.

While Ivy may be happy with a non-traditional wedding, she was adamant about sticking to the tradition of not seeing each other the night before the ceremony. It's bad luck, apparently. I don't believe in bad luck—I believe you make your own luck. It's an unshakeable belief that's put me at the top of my profession.

I wasn't happy about being away from Ivy for twenty-four hours, but it was important to her. And there's nothing I won't do for my soon-to-be-wife. So, last night was the first time we didn't sleep in the same bed since I brought her to my apartment three months ago.

Three months of fucking bliss with the woman who owns every part of me. I'd move heaven and earth to see her beautiful smile. And I'd sell my soul to the devil to ensure she's safe because there is no me without her.

I shove my shaking hands into the pockets of my expensive suit while I wait for Ivy and Kathy to arrive. Kathy took me to one side to give me her blessing when I dropped Ivy off at her house two days ago. It lifted a weight from my shoulders I didn't realize I was carrying. The last little splinter of guilt has been removed, and I'm ready to claim the woman I love.

As if my thoughts have summoned her, I turn to see Ivy walking toward me. She's a fucking vision in a white dress that clings to her curves and shows a hint of her generous cleavage. My God, she's stunning. She steals my breath, weakens my knees, and hardens my cock.

The primal part of me that's always close to the surface when it comes to Ivy wants to rip that dress from her gorgeous body and slide home—because she is my home. We've had each other in every conceivable position during the past three months, but our desire for each other is never sated for long.

All her emotions are laid bare in her honey-brown eyes as they fix on mine—happiness, desire, excitement, but above all, love. We fit. It's as simple as that.

She smiles at me, and I'm complete.

Time to make her my wife.

# Epilogue 2
## Ivy

My entire life has led up to this moment.

I was made to be Ashton's wife.

My eyes fall on him, and my breath stalls in my lungs. He's the most handsome man I've ever known. His suit fits him to perfection, making my mouth water. His eyes kindle as they take me in, skimming over my curves in my simple white dress.

I can barely believe I'm marrying the man of my dreams. Ashton Stanbrook is about to become my husband. I spent so long loving him from a distance, it seems surreal.

"You look so beautiful," he growls as I reach him, my mom at my side.

She's fussed and primped me to within an inch of my life over the last few hours. It's been wonderful spending some time together. I know she was initially opposed to this union, but she's come around now that she sees how much Ash and I love each other. The fact that she's here by my side on my wedding day speaks volumes.

"So do you," I murmur, smiling so hard my cheeks hurt. My heart is overflowing with love for this passionate, growly, possessive man who's given me so much.

I give him a smirk. "Wanna get married?"

He reaches for my hand. "Thought you'd never ask."

I squeeze his hand, elation flooding my entire body so it feels like I'm walking on air.

The wedding ceremony is short, poignant, and perfect. I lose myself in Ash's eyes as we say our vows, our words crafted with love and spoken straight from the heart.

Ashton carries me over the threshold into our hotel room, an exquisite suite he's booked for two nights before we head off on our honeymoon to Europe.

"This is crazy," I murmur as he places me on the enormous bed.

Ash frowns. "Crazy, how?"

"I've loved you for an eternity, never dreaming you'd be mine, yet here we are, husband and wife, planning a future together. I can't wait to do all the things with you. You're my wisdom, my heart"—I pause, cupping his face in my hands as he leans over me—"my Ashton."

He turns his face, kissing my palm. "And you're my fucking everything, Mrs. Stanbrook. From now to the grave."

Tears spill down my cheeks as I pull him to me, claiming his mouth in a breathless kiss. Sparks ignite in my core, and I'm suddenly desperate for him.

"I need you," I breathe against his mouth.

"You got me, Kitten," he growls, kissing me hard.

In no time, we're naked, his cock pressing against my entrance.

"I love you, wife," he mutters as he thrusts inside me.

"Love you, husband. Now, fuck me hard."

He does as I ask, slamming inside me with a primal growl. I cry out in ecstasy, clinging to him, breathless with pleasure.

I'm ready for our future.

I'm ready for it all.

# Bonus Scene 1
## Ashton

**Five Years Later...**

"Daddy, me hungwy!"

I look down at Jake, his blonde hair curling around his forehead and ears. He rubs a chubby hand over his stomach, looking at me with big, hazel-brown eyes, the same shade as his mama's.

"You're always hungry, squirt!" I reply, swinging him up into my arms and kissing his cheek. "Don't worry. Mommy's on her way with takeout."

"Me like buggers!" Jake says with a toothy smile. He's almost two years old and the light of our lives.

I laugh at his mispronunciation. "I think you mean burgers!"

"Wiv cheese and fwies," he nods enthusiastically.

"Is there any other way to eat them?" I ask seriously.

"And 'mato ketchup!" he announces, throwing his arms wide.

He's so damn cute, but that's to be expected since he looks just like his beautiful mama. He has the same ability to brighten up a room like Ivy does. But one thing he's inherited from me is his appetite. He's always hungry.

I'm always hungry too, but most of the time, it's for my wife. She's only grown more beautiful during the last five years, and when she was pregnant with Jake, I couldn't keep my fucking hands off her. Not that she minded. She craves my cock like I crave every precious inch of her.

Which is why she's pregnant again. I'm forty-four years old, but she makes me feel like a horny teenager. My favorite place to be is inside her tight, wet pussy.

Today is our fifth wedding anniversary. Kathy is coming by to babysit her grandson while I take my wife out for a candlelit dinner for two at her favorite Italian restaurant. She works damn hard as a pediatric nurse, and she deserves a little pampering.

Which is why she's grabbing takeout for the little monster on her way home. Jake wanted to come with us tonight, so we blackmailed him with his favorite "bugger and fwies"—not something we often do, but tonight is our night. No little third wheels, no matter how cute he is. Besides, he loves his Grandma Kathy, and she adores him, spoiling him rotten with her time and attention.

"I'm home!" a voice calls, followed by the sound of the front door closing. "Is there someone here who likes cheeseburgers?"

"Me!" Jake shouts, wriggling out of my arms and making a beeline for his mama as she enters the living room.

She's wearing her usual work uniform of black pants and tunic. The tunic is colorful, printed with cartoon characters, making her more relatable to the kids she works with. I love that she's doing a job she adores and finds so rewarding. I decided to reduce my hours at my construction company to take care of Jake. I wouldn't trade the last two years with my son for anything.

"Hey, munchkin!" Ivy grins, crouching down to scoop him up. She buries her nose in his neck, and he giggles. "I missed you today."

"Did you miss me, too?" I ask with a quirk of my eyebrow.

"I always miss you," Ivy replies, giving me a meaningful glance over our son's head.

My eyes drop to her swollen belly. Three more months until we get to meet our daughter. Fuck, she's sexy when she's carrying my babies. Her eyes catch fire at the look in mine, and I know she's going to ride me like a rodeo queen later.

Her tawny eyes darken, and she licks her lips. Okay, maybe sooner rather than later. My woman is even hornier when she's pregnant, much to my delight.

We sit opposite Jake at the dining table while he eats, catching up on each other's day while he chatters away in the background. I massage her lower back as I sit next to her, watching with pleasure as goosebumps rise on her arms. She's as affected by my touch now as she was our first time together. It humbles me.

I move my hand further down, teasing the sensitive spot right at the base of her spine that drives her crazy. Her breath catches, and her nipples stiffen beneath her tunic. I can't help the tiny growl that escapes my throat. I want them in my mouth so I can lick and bite them until she's squirming and panting for me.

My cock is throbbing behind the seam of my jeans. He needs to satisfy himself in one of her pretty little holes. He's not fussy about which one, and neither is Ivy. I'm not sure where she loves my cock best, in her tight pussy, her pretty mouth, or pumping into her ass.

"All done!" Jake announces happily, a smear of tomato ketchup across his cheek as he shows us his empty plate.

"I think you inhaled that!" Ivy smiles, moving away to pluck Jake from his booster seat while I clear up after him.

"Can I watch Paw Patrol, Mama?" he asks, settling hopeful brown eyes on her.

"Go wash up, and I'll put it on for you," she nods, setting him on his feet and watching affectionately as he waddles off to the bathroom.

Her eyes snap to me, alive with desire. "Think you can come up with something creative in the bedroom for ten minutes while he watches his favorite cartoon?"

# Bonus Scene 2
## Ivy

My husband doesn't need to be asked twice. The second Jake is safely distracted in front of the TV, he manhandles me into the bedroom, turning the lock we had fitted when Jake started to walk. Jake may have forgotten interrupting Mommy and Daddy's playtime when he came in rubbing his eyes sleepily after a bad dream one night, but we haven't. The lock went on the very next morning.

But right now, I have my hot husband to myself for ten minutes, and I don't want to waste a single one of them.

We make quick work of our clothing, and then Ash is on me, his mouth on mine, our tongues swirling hungrily together. He trails a hand up my thigh and cups my pussy, feeling the slickness that coats my inner thighs.

"Wet for me already, Kitten?" he mutters, sliding his mouth along my jaw and biting my earlobe.

My body clenches with need. "I'm always wet for you, Ash," I gasp as his fingers slip inside me.

I'm a lucky girl. My husband is still the sexiest man I've ever laid eyes on, and he worships the ground I walk on. He has a little more gray threaded through his hair these days, but he's in great shape and more handsome than ever. He just improves with every year that passes, aging like the finest of wines.

My pregnant belly protrudes between us, but Ash doesn't seem to care. If anything, seeing our baby growing in my belly turns him into a grunting, horny Neanderthal. Which is fine by me.

"God, you get more beautiful every day," he breathes, smoothing his hands over my stomach and cupping my heavy breasts.

"Ash?"

"Yeah, Kitten?"

"Stop talking and fuck me."

He pulls back to look at me with that cocky smirk I love so much. "You got it, baby. But later tonight, after I've wined and dined you, I'm going to make you beg for my cock again."

I nod enthusiastically. "Deal!"

I want that. Most of the time, he treats me like a precious

gem, but in the bedroom, he's an animal. And I love it. I crave it. Just like I crave him.

He sits on the edge of the bed, his cock standing proud with its bead of precum moistening the head. "Climb on, Kitten."

My pussy clenches and I do as he asks, positioning myself over his lap so that his cock is notched at my entrance. His hands move to my hips, holding me steady, and then I slam myself down on his engorged length. We both moan at the heady sensation. It's the same every time. We fit like puzzle pieces.

Ash takes me roughly, supporting my weight as he bounces me up and down on his thick cock. His mouth latches onto my breast, and I bite off a moan as he suckles hard at my nipple. My pussy walls clench around him, creating the perfect sheath to milk his cum from him.

"Fuck, Ivy!" he grunts, his hips moving like pistons as he thrusts harder and harder.

I match him, undulating my hips against his so that our bodies come together with wet slaps. I know he's getting close. I can feel it in the desperation of his movements, the set of his jaw, the bite of his fingers into my hips.

"Come for me, Ash," I demand, squeezing my internal muscles around him.

A deep rumble works its way up from his chest to his throat, and his face contorts. His hands pin my hips to his length tightly as his cock twitches and pulses inside me. Nothing does it for me like the sensation of his cum filling me up. Watching him go over the edge always triggers my orgasm. I grind myself against him, head back, body arched as I chant his name.

I slump against him as the last tendrils of pleasure fade away. Ash nuzzles his face against my throat while his hands caress my baby bump.

"How did I do?" he asks, sliding his tongue lazily over my nipple and making me shiver.

I glance at the clock on the bedside table. "Eight minutes, give or take," I say with a satisfied smile.

"Damn, I'm good." He grins, spearing his hands through my hair and pulling my head down for his kiss. It's tender, poignant, full of everything he feels for me.

I sigh, wrapping my arms around him, savoring these precious moments in his arms. "Happy anniversary, darling. Thank you for being an amazing husband and a wonderful father. I love you so much."

He tips his head back to look up at me, his blue eyes glittering with emotion. "Love you, too, Mrs. Stanbrook. Always will. And I can't wait to show you again later."

"Mommy? Daddy?" The door handle rattles as Jake tries to get in.

I smile and lean down to kiss my husband. "Hold that thought."

---

Thank you for reading!

Reviews help readers discover new books! If you enjoyed **Claiming Ivy**, I'd love to hear what you enjoyed most—your review means the world to me and guides other readers to discover my work.

Thanks for choosing my stories—I hope they allow you to escape and relax for a few hours.

Love,

Violet.

**Keep reading for an excerpt from Claiming Lily…**

# Claiming Lily Sneak Peek

**He has everything money can buy—except her heart. Can they keep things professional, or will desire take control?**

**Callum**

I've built my IT empire from scratch, earning my place as one of San Antonio's youngest billionaires by thirty. I've got everything money can buy—except the love of a good woman. Then Lily walks into my office with those hazel-green eyes and curves that make my pulse race. Hiring her as my assistant was easy. Convincing her we're meant to be? That's the challenge I'm ready to take on.

**Lily**

Getting hired by Callum Rogen, tech genius and heart-throb billionaire, should be a dream. But with sparks flying every time he looks my way, keeping things professional is proving impossible. He's everything I've ever wanted—and the one thing I shouldn't have. It's only a matter of time before we cross the line from business to pleasure... and I'm not sure I want to stop.

## Sneak Peek

## Callum

I lean back in my leather chair with a sigh, scrubbing a weary hand over my face.

How hard can it be to find a new personal assistant? I've interviewed ten people today alone, men and women alike, and none of them have been a good fit for me or my company. Three of the interviewees practically propositioned me for the job. I've built my billion-dollar IT company through a combination of hard work and determination, and I'm tired of people who think they can suck or fuck their way up the career ladder.

I swivel my chair towards the computer screen, pulling up the *résumé* for the next interviewee. Mary, my current personal assistant, has vetted them all and arranged the interviews for suitable candidates, so I only give it a cursory scan.

Lily Olsen, twenty-four years old, business degree, qualifying with honors. Two previous employers, both construction companies, based in Houston. She only worked for the latter, Miller Corp., for three months.

I frown, wondering why Mary has put someone through for an interview who has no experience in the IT field. I need someone who knows their way around this industry. Looks like this is going to be a short interview.

Releasing another heavy sigh, I press the intercom on the desk phone with a distinct lack of enthusiasm. "Send Miss. Olsen in, please, Mary."

"Of course. She's your last one today," Mary's disembodied voice replies.

*Thank fuck.*

Mary is retiring in less than a week, and I still haven't found the right person to fill her shoes, despite interviewing candidates for the last two days straight.

A firm rap on the door pulls my attention from the computer screen. "Come in!"

The door opens, and I rise automatically from my chair, a polite smile fixed on my face. The smile freezes in place when a woman I can only describe as a curvy goddess floats into my office.

She's beautiful. Stunning. Above-average height, maybe five-eight, but I've still got several inches on her. Striking hazel-green eyes, cute nose, full pink lips. Her dark hair is pulled into a soft bun, with a few tendrils floating around her flushed cheeks. She's wearing a black skirt that flares to just below her knees, with a silky blue blouse that complements her coloring. Her choice of clothes is entirely suitable for an interview but draped over her delicious curves, they look fucking spectacular.

She clears her throat. "Um, Mr. Rogen?"

I blink, suddenly realizing she's waiting for me to enunciate actual words—difficult to do when my bottom lip is trailing on the floor.

I clear my throat. "Sorry. Been a long day already." I hold out my hand to her. "Please, call me Callum. Nice to meet you, Miss. Olsen."

"Lily," she says, placing her hand in mine.

Her handshake is firm, and the feel of her soft skin sends a bolt of electricity straight to my balls. I hold her hand just a fraction too long, reluctant to break the physical contact.

Ah, fuck. I'm in so much trouble. Any idea I had of this being a short interview has just evaporated in a puff of lust.

*Hypocrite.*

Yeah, I am, but what can I say? I'm a stubborn fucker when I see something I want. I haven't even started the interview yet, and I'm already planning how to get this curvy angel into my life and my bed and keep her there.

"Please. Sit," I offer, indicating the chair in front of my desk.

I return to my seat, watching as Lily perches on the chair, tucking her skirt neatly beneath her before clasping her hands in her lap.

"Would you like something to drink? Coffee? Tea? Water?" I ask.

"No, thank you. I ate lunch not long ago, so I'm good, thanks. Besides, coffee and tea make me want to pee and —" she stops abruptly, looking mortified. "Sorry. Too much information. I tend to babble when I'm nervous, and the filter between my brain and my mouth stops working."

Jesus, she's too fucking cute.

"It's fine," I chuckle, waving it off. "Coffee has the same effect on me."

Lily smiles. "I'm sure that's not true, but thanks for trying to make me feel better."

I can't take my eyes off her. When she smiles, she does it with her whole face, eyes sparkling, cute nose scrunched up, full mouth stretched wide. I wonder what it would look like stretched wide around my aching cock.

"So, uh, tell me a little about yourself, Lily. Are you married? Children?" I ask casually, trying to ignore the massive boner straining against my pants.

"Not married. No kids," she replies. "Just me and Groot."

"Groot?"

"My cat. I named him after the character from Guardians of the Galaxy. I'm a huge Marvel movie geek," she admits sheepishly.

"Sci-Fi's not my thing," I reply, making a mental note to download every fucking one of those movies the first chance I get. "So, what made you apply for this position? Your resume shows that your previous job was with Miller Corp. in Houston. What brings you to San Antonio?"

Lily looks uncomfortable for a split second before summoning a bright smile. "I, uh, needed a change of scenery. I grew up just outside Houston. My biological father died before I was born, so it was just Mom and me until I was eight when she met Joe. He adopted me when they got married. He's a good man and the only dad I've ever known. When Joe and Mom moved to California with his job, I decided to stay in Houston. I shared an apartment with Daisy, my best friend, but she had to move back to Colorado, so it seemed like a good time to try my luck in San Antonio and—" she stops abruptly. "Oh, my God, I'm so sorry. I'm babbling again. Daisy's always saying I can talk the legs off a chair," she grimaces, biting her plump bottom lip.

Fuck. Just when I thought she couldn't get any more adorable.

"Sounds like your mom found a good man in your step-dad. I lost both my parents eight years ago in a car accident," I say, the words spilling from my lips before I can stop them.

*The fuck?* I never talk about my parents. It's still too painful. This woman is casting a spell on me, making me feel like I can share anything with her.

"I'm sorry. It never leaves you, does it, the grief of losing loved ones? You just make room for it," she says with wisdom beyond her years. "You were obviously close."

"We were. They never got to see all this." I wave a hand around me to encompass the business I've built. "They were happily married for thirty years. They only had eyes for each other. Dad treated Mom like a queen, and she thought the sun rose and set on him. They lived their lives by a solid moral compass, and they instilled those values in my brother and me, taught us that success comes with hard work and determination. Which is why I won't ever forget my roots, where I came from."

"So you're not the kind of billionaire who lounges on yachts sipping champagne or dines on caviar in Michelin-star restaurants, huh?" she asks playfully.

I grin. "Give me a dirty cheeseburger any day."

Lily returns my smile. "Man after my own heart."

Jesus, if only she knew just how close to the mark that statement is—because I think I might be after her heart.

She's weaving her magic around me, making me all fucking warm and gooey inside.

"So, why did you leave your previous job?" I ask, forcing my attention back to business.

Her smile disappears, and she looks oddly nervous again. "It was a great company to work for, but I felt I wasn't being utilized to my full potential."

Her words sound stilted, like she's been practicing them in front of a mirror.

"You haven't worked in IT before," I say, pointing out the obvious.

Lily purses her lips thoughtfully. "That's true, but my skills are transferable to any business. I've done my research, Mr. Rog—Callum. I know you've built this company from the ground up, and you developed a new type of angular programming with almost zero rework and less code required whenever a new feature is added. You've encompassed languages and tools for Ruby, HTML, PHP, Perl, and Pascal as standard in your package. I'm so confident I'll be an asset to you and your company that I'm prepared to work my first month for free."

I stare at her. Fuck, she's hot when she's talking about rework and coding. She's my dream woman. All I can think about is bending her over my desk, fisting my hand in her hair, and sliding into her wet warmth.

"That won't be necessary," I say gruffly, glad the desk hides my massive erection. "When can you start?"

Lily's mouth drops open. "Huh?"

"The job is yours. When can you start?" I repeat.

"But—you've barely asked me any questions. Don't you want to know about my office skills? Interview the rest of the candidates?"

"I've spent the last two days interviewing candidates, Lily. None of them instilled the confidence in me that you have in less than five minutes. I'm a damned good judge of character. I've had to be to get where I am. I'm a workaholic. I don't expect the same level of dedication from my employees because that would involve living, eating, and sleeping the job, but I do expect hard work, loyalty, and dedication. The job is demanding, and as my assistant, there will be the occasional business trip, which you'll be required to accompany me on, and for which you will be well reimbursed. So if this sounds like something you can handle, the job is yours."

"Yes, I can handle you," she says enthusiastically. "I mean, the job. I can handle the job," she amends quickly, her cheeks turning pink.

I bite back a smile. "Good. Can you start next Monday?"

She bobs her head in a vigorous nod, causing a few more tendrils of silky hair to break loose from her bun to frame her lovely face. "I don't know what to say. Thank you so much. You won't regret it, I promise."

She's right. I won't regret it. The only thing I'd regret is letting her walk out of my office and never seeing her again. Lily doesn't know it yet, but she's just been claimed. Not for one night. Not for a few weeks. I'm claiming her for life.

# About the Author

**Loved this book?**

**Find more steamy romances from Violet Rae:**

Author Violet Rae

Violet Rae writes spicy, emotionally charged romances where the connection is instant, the heroes are protective (and a little bit unhinged for their woman), and the heat level threatens to set off smoke alarms. From fated mates in outer space to small-town rescues and paranormal standoffs, Violet's stories deliver fast love, fierce devotion, and that delicious fantasy of being utterly cherished.

There's always a woman in danger (or simply in need of a serious nap), a hero who will burn down the world for her, and just enough humor to make you snort-laugh between kisses and kidnappings. Found families, caretaking intimacy, dirty talk, and happily-ever-afters are guaranteed—along with a little chaos, a lot of heart, and the kind of chemistry that makes your eReader blush.

**Fast love. Fierce devotion. Delicious fantasies.**

*Violet is the original creator of the following multi author series':*

*Monster Between the Sheets*

*Dad Bod: Men Built for Comfort*

*Dad Bod: Large and in Charge*

*Dad Bod: Christmas*

*Dad Bod: Monster Edition*

*Filthy Fairy Tales*